True Friends

CARMEN BROWNE SERIES #1

True Friends

Stephanie Perry Moore

MOODY PUBLISHERS
CHICAGO

All Scripture quotatons are taken from the King James Version.

ISBN: 0-8024-8172-8
EAN/ISBN-13: 978-08024-8172-6

Library of Congress Cataloging-in-Publication Data

Moore, Stephanie Perry.
    True friends / by Stephanie Perry Moore.
        p. cm. — (Carmen Browne series ; bk. #1)
    Summary: When her African-American family moves to a new town after her father takes a football coaching job at a historically black university, ten-year-old Carmen learns important lessons about friendship and prejudice.
    ISBN 0-8024-8172-8
    [1. Friendship—Fiction. 2. Prejudices—Fiction. 3. Moving, Household—Fiction. 4. African Americans—Fiction. 5. Christian life—Fiction. 6. Virginia—Fiction.] I. Title.

PZ7.M788125Tr 2005
[Fic]--dc22

                                            2004019892

3 5 7 9 10 8 6 4

Printed in the United States of America

To my fifth-grade buddies

Amber Michelle Jarrett
and
Vickie Lynn Randall,

whose friendships
I now truly see
I didn't always deserve.
Because of those memories,
maybe I can help other adolescent girls
avoid the mistakes
I made!

Thanks for loving me anyway.

Contents

Acknowledgments

I was supposed to proof my story today
and have it back to the Moody editor, but
I couldn't work on it. We had some trees
down in our yard from the storm, I had to
help my daughter with a social studies project, and I really needed to finish working
on a Bible project. So, missing my deadline,
I was bummed.

However, four of my dear friends took
me out to the spa. We had such a good time,
laughing at nothing and lifting each other
up. With good friends on your side, life is
sooooo much better. Being twenty-five years
older than the character in this book, I'd say
I know quite a lot about true friendships.
Two important things I know is that you

have to treat a friend as you want to be treated and I've also learned that you can't take them for granted. Having said that, here's a small bit of thanks to all who helped me get this book published.

To my parents, Dr. Franklin and Shirley Perry, thanks for always being not just a parent, but a friend. I hope you're proud of your little girl.

To my Moody Team, especially Greg Thornton, Matt Parker, and Cynthia Ballenger, you've taken a chance on my writing once again. I'm so grateful.

To my dear spa friends, Taiwanna Bolds, Deborah Bradley, Jackie Dixon, and Tabatha Palmer, your support gets me through. With friends like you, I'm a blessed woman.

To my daughters, Syndi and Sheldyn, finally Mommy wrote a book for you two. Just doing your best and treating people right makes me proud.

To my hubby, Derrick Moore, ten years of enduring friendship. God has been good to us.

To my new young readers, praying this book is as good as a Disney movie and as filling as your mom's best meal. Take in the words.

And to my Lord, finally my desire for this series matched Your perfect timing. Thank You for being my closest friend. I hope these young readers find You early.

1

Lost Vision

Heavenly Father, I know I'm not seeing right, I prayed as I stood in the family room listening to my parents discuss what had to be the worst news of my almost ten years of life. *Dear God, please help!*

"Dad," I said, "there's no way we can move. You can't coach at Virginia State. My life is here!" I yelled loudly, as if my forceful tone would change my father's mind.

Placing one hand on my shoulder, Dad gently replied, "Calm down, Carmen. I know Charlottesville has been your home all your life, but it's time to move on."

"I don't want to move on! This isn't fair," I argued, stepping away.

"Now, just a minute, young lady," my

dad, Charles Browne, said with a stern face. "You aren't the only one who has to make a sacrifice. All of us—your mother, your brother, and your little sister—will be giving up things as well. If it weren't a good opportunity, I wouldn't even be moving our family. Besides, we're not even leaving the state. You'll love Ettrick."

I dashed to my room, burst into tears, and threw myself on my canopy bed. How could my parents be so insensitive? Ever since I was in kindergarten, I'd been waiting for the day that I could run the school as a sixth grader. My year was finally approaching. I was just one year away. Now I had to move. Why was my life so crazy? *Why, Lord?*

I rolled over and stared from beneath my canopy at the bright white ceiling and the banana-colored walls. With my arms folded defiantly across my chest, I cried aloud, "Well, I'm not going. I'll ask Jillian's parents if I can live with them till I graduate from high school. I'm over there all the time anyway."

My best friend, Jillian Gray, and I were inseparable. I hoped the Grays would love to have me as part of their family.

As I thought of a change in my surroundings, I hit the pillow to let out my frustrations. "Jillian would make a better sister than the one I've got anyway," I grumbled.

For one thing, I wouldn't have to worry about Jillian going into my stuff all the time, like my eight-year-old sister, Cassie, did. That morning she'd broken my gold chain, which she had no business wearing in the first place. When I caught her with it on, she pulled it off real quick.

It was also annoying that Cassie used my hair grease. I wouldn't have to worry about that with Jillian. She wasn't black like me. Jillian was white. She told me that her hair was so straight and fine with natural oil, so she didn't need to use any.

Since Jillian was an only child, I wouldn't have to worry about an older brother. Every time I tried to watch television, my irritating brother, Clay, came in and changed the channel. He just surfed from station to station, not really watching anything. And he picked on me about everything. Yeah, I could definitely do without his big twelve-year-old mouth.

My folks wouldn't miss me anyway. After a year, Mom's at-home business was finally taking off. She was a visual artist and did pretty well at selling her paintings. My father was an assistant football coach for the University of Virginia. When it was football season, he was hardly ever around. With me gone, they'd have one less kid to worry about.

After about twenty minutes, I had completely sold myself on the idea. Now all I had to do was come up with a plan.

✪

After dinner, my family headed to the garage to pack up stuff in there, but thankfully I didn't have to help. Since my mother knew I was sad about the move, she encouraged Dad to let me stay in my room. This would be my time to think without them nearby.

As soon as they went to the garage, I started packing. I couldn't take everything, but some items were essential. I stuffed my CDs, posters, headset, my Bible, and a few of my favorite clothes in two suitcases.

Writing a letter explaining my disappearance was next. But that was tough. Everything I felt inside sounded wrong when I wrote it down on paper and read it back to myself.

After several rushed attempts, I came up with this:

Dear Family,

I love you all, but I cannot, will not, should not move. So I'm running away. Don't worry about me. I'll be fine. You all move on and I will see you if you come back to visit. That is, if I don't have other plans. Take care of each other.

Carmen

✪

Gazing around my room, I almost had second thoughts. *How could I run away?* I wondered. Quickly, I realized that it was no time to get all mushy. It was now or never. I picked up the two suitcases, jetted through the hall, opened the front door, and locked the wooden door. I dashed past my closed garage, hoping it would not open. Then I rushed two houses down to Jillian's.

I rang the doorbell ten times, hoping someone would open it. When that never happened, I hated that I hadn't called first. If I kept standing there on the front porch, my parents would spot me. So I marched around to the back-yard and sat on the redwood deck.

A few minutes later, I heard a car pull up out front. I peeked around the corner of the house and saw Mr. and Mrs. Gray pulling into the driveway in their pretty new white Jeep. When I saw them unload a few bags from stores in the mall, I realized they had just gone shopping. My best friend's parents were so cool. They always bought her tons of clothes. I knew they'd do the same for me if I lived with them.

"Jillian," I whispered loudly, peeking from around the bushes as she started following her parents inside. When she turned and saw me, I said, "I need your help."

My friend was taller than me. She had short straw-berry blonde hair. Big freckles covered her face. We had been close since nursery school, but I'd never needed her more than that moment.

Jillian snuck over to where I was hiding. "Carmen, what's wrong?"

"I need to stay here until I graduate from high school," I confided.

"What are you talking about?" she asked.

I pointed to my suitcases, still sitting on the deck. "Help me get my things inside, and I'll explain everything."

As we stretched across Jillian's bed, I told her about the move. We both started weeping.

"I can't imagine a world without you in it," she wailed. "Of course you can move in with me."

We spent about an hour talking about how cool it would be to be sisters. Exchanging secrets until dawn would make our every-night slumber parties extra fun.

"Let's go tell my parents," Jillian suggested. "I'm sure they'll be okay with you living here."

As we started down the stairs, I heard the angry voice of my father. Jillian and I stopped on the fifth step from the bottom, listening to him rant and rave. All of our excitement vanished.

"I've got to get my stuff and get out of here," I told Jillian in a panicky whisper.

"Where will you go?" my friend asked, her eyes wide.

I had no answer. My grandparents all lived in Durham, North Carolina. And I didn't have any other close friends.

Taking a deep breath, I took the last five steps and bravely entered the living room. My mother threw her arms around me the instant she saw me. I felt sorry for causing her pain. My stomach ached as bad as if I had the flu.

"Oh, baby," Mom gasped with relief. "I'm so glad you're safe."

"I'm okay, Ma," I said, wiggling out of her hug. "I'm sorry I worried you. I just thought—"

My father cut me off. "That's the problem—you didn't think. Carmen, I am sick of this foolishness. Get your things right now, say good-bye to Jillian, and let's go home."

"But Dad, I—"

"Close your mouth right now, Carmen Lynn Browne! Do not say one more word. We'll talk about this at home." My father opened the Grays' back door. Mom mumbled something to Mr. and Mrs. Gray.

I looked at Jillian, then followed my parents, wishing this wasn't happening to me.

✪

I was put on punishment for a week. No phone, no friends, and no television. My father said I was acting too grown-up and needed to be reminded who was in charge.

Those seven days were spent packing boxes of stuff. That was even harder to take than the grounding. It finally hit me that I was leaving my entire world behind.

As I pouted in my bedroom, while looking at my fourth-grade yearbook, my little sister came in—without knocking, as usual. She held out a cherry Popsicle toward me, cherry juice dripping through her fingers.

I just stared at her for a while. For the most part, Cassie was a good sister. Even though she got on my nerves, I still loved her.

I finally took the Popsicle, smiled, and said, "You're being awful sweet."

"I don't want to move either," she said. "But if I have to go, I want you to go too."

What a cool thing to say! When I first thought of living with Jillian and her family, I thought no one would miss me. At least my little sister cared.

"Cassie," my dad called from the doorway, "please go downstairs and help your brother pack the videos. We need to speak to your sister alone."

As my sister scurried out, I saw my mom standing behind my father. They both came in and sat on my bed, leaving no space between them.

I had been a perfect angel on punishment, but as I sat down, I felt nervous. Their faces looked serious. Maybe they were going to extend my suffering.

"Mom . . . Dad," I said, "I want to apologize for being such a bother lately."

"Looks like you've been busy in here." I looked around my bare-walled room. Labeled boxes covered the floor. "You go, girl." My dad gave me a high five, finally turning back into the cool, fun, laid-back dad I was used to.

My mother put her arm around me. "Since next week is the Fourth of July and your tenth birthday, your father and I thought you might want to have a party. It would be a nice way to say good-bye to your friends."

"Thanks!" I said, a huge grin plastered across my face.

As soon as they left my room, I started making my invitation list. I included every friend I had.

I started to feel better about my parents. I knew Dad didn't want to move any more than the rest of us. He was just trying his best to provide a good living for us. Now opportunity was having us knock on a different door.

My dad had been involved in sports all his life. He'd graduated from the University of North Carolina with a degree in physical education, and then he became an all-pro wide receiver for the Washington Redskins.

For the last five years, he had been a coach at the University of Virginia. I remembered him telling me that it took more than his abilities and qualifications to land that job. I was only five years old at the time, so I didn't understand what he meant. I still didn't get it. What team wouldn't want a man who'd played three years in the National Football League? People love being around pro players. All I knew was that my dad wanted a promotion, and he didn't get it. I prayed that maybe one day the blanks of the story would be filled in.

✪

The days passed slowly, and yet every time I thought about moving day, it didn't feel like I had enough time.

When the day of my party finally arrived, Jillian came over to help set up. Hanging pink and yellow balloons and streamers all over the family room reminded us of all the parties we'd had together over the years. Even though I was the only black girl in our class, Jillian never made me feel different.

"Jillian," I said as we put paper plates and cups on the table, "I prayed to God last night that you and I will always be friends. I know we won't be able to talk every day on the phone, have slumber parties all the time, or walk down the hallways together at school. It would just be nice to have a friend like you in my life forever."

"Well, Miss Serious, as long as I have breath you'll have me as a friend," she said jokingly, letting loose into my face the air of a balloon she'd just blown up.

My guests started arriving right at five o'clock. Clay and Cassie got to invite a few of their friends too. When Mom said I had to share the party with my brother and sister, I started to protest. Then I realized it wasn't just my birthday party. The three of us were celebrating things that would never be, at least not here in Charlottesville. No going to the skating rinks with these people. No spring breaks to fill with fun, and no more summers together.

Everybody had a fun time. Music and laughter filled our house one last time. I walked over to Mom and brushed a tear from her flushed cheeks.

"Pumpkin," she said to me, "I'm so glad you're having

a wonderful time. It's good to see a smile on your face. I know you still have reservations about moving, but I promise you . . . I'll do whatever I can to help make your adjustment easy."

I hugged her, and as I watched her walk away, I kept her last words with me. I wasn't ready to move, but I now realized there was no way I could stay someplace without my family. My home was wherever my dad, mom, Clay, and Cassie lived. Home wasn't only a city or a house. Home—my home—was in love. I was just thankful the Lord let me see; I no longer had lost vision.

2

Blind Faith

During our first two weeks of living in Ettrick, Virginia, about two hours south of my old hometown, we still hadn't had a chance to get out and explore our new surroundings. The weather had been bad. The days were so dark and cloudy, no kids played outside. The hard thunder and lightning had kept my family in the windowless bathroom most nights.

One family's house in our new neighborhood caught on fire when lightning struck the roof. It caused a blast of flames on the top level. Good thing, no one was hurt. After the storm passed, we heard on the news that twelve people in the area lost their lives. We prayed for those victims and their families. I must admit, it was difficult feeling sadness for people I didn't know. But when I remembered how afraid I felt night after night, it was easy to relate to the pain those strangers went through.

I wasn't crazy about being in this new place, but surviving the storm gave me another outlook on my situation. I was alive! Mom said God spared our lives for a purpose. Although I couldn't see the reason, I was thankful for another day—even if it was in Ettrick, Virginia.

✪

"Finally, we're out of the house!" my sister screamed with joy to my brother and me.

The three of us headed to the corner store. Our mission was to buy Popsicles to fight off the ninety-six-degree heat. I wish I could've hung out with friends, but since we knew no one in the area, Clay, my bookworm brother, and Cassie, my bothersome sister, had become my best friends.

London's Grocery was farther away than we thought. Cassie started complaining about being tired. Even though her whining was annoying, I was worn out too. So I suggested we call Mom to come get us. Clay, trying to be tough, said we could take the shortcut home.

"What shortcut?" I asked my brother.

"The path through the woods over there," Clay replied confidently. "It has to lead to our neighborhood.

See . . . look down the path. The dirt curves toward where we live."

"I don't want to go through there," Cassie said, holding Clay's arm tightly. "A snake might get us. And those bushes are thick. It looks too dark and scary."

Dark and *scary* were definitely words I'd use to describe that gloomy route. With all the brains Clay had, I didn't know why he was crazy enough to think I'd be willing to travel that unknown road. Nevertheless, he finally convinced me and Cassie to trust him. He promised to lead us home safely and quickly.

"It only makes sense to go this way," he continued to argue as we followed him into the woods. "The shortest distance between two points is a straight line."

The shaded path was cool, at least. And no strange insects bothered us. All we heard was the peaceful chirping of three robins nestled on some branches.

All of a sudden I smelled something weird in the air. For a second, I thought it might be a fire. But the odor was stronger than regular smoke. The view in front of us changed from clear to cloudy.

"You guys smell that?" I asked my brother and sister.

"Yeah." Cassie coughed. "I can hardly breathe."

As we inched closer to the origin of the smoke, we noticed three boys. They had to be teenagers, because they were big. They looked kinda rough and tough. They were arguing with one another over something. I didn't want to find out what.

"Get off me, man," the shortest of the three said to his buddy in a panic. "Look over there. Someone's checkin' us out. Quick, put it out."

I started to turn back and take my little sister with me. But the boys spotted us, and we froze. I stopped dead in my tracks as a tall, dark-skinned, bald-headed, buff guy walked up to my brother and asked, "Hey, lil' homey, what you doin' out here? Ain't you scared of the boogeyman? Or snakes?"

Cassie peeked from behind Clay and asked, "Are there snakes out here?"

"There's one, lil' sista . . . me. My name is Snake. And you kids better be worried about me. If you ever sneak up on me and my crew again, I'll bite."

I didn't know much about gangs, violence, alcohol, or drugs. Our parents never let us watch violent stuff on television. In Charlottesville, where we moved from, we didn't see a lot of rough kids or gangs. I figured Snake must have been this boy's code name, nickname, or gang name. Surely his mother wouldn't name him that.

Every part of me wanted to run away. But the three of them made a triangle around us.

Snake held a short, white, smoking object in front of Clay. It looked a little like a cigarette. Snake asked my brother if he wanted to take "a hit."

Despite the fear on Clay's face, he stood up to Snake and said, "Naw, man, thanks . . . but no thanks. If y'all don't mind, my sisters and I are just trying to find our way home."

Clay tried to walk around them, motioning Cassie and me to follow. I stood still when the big guy cut off our path.

"No one says no to Snake," he snarled. "Quit actin' like a punk."

"Just let us get by. You won't have to worry about seeing us again."

"Where do y'all live?" Snake pried.

I did not want this bully knowing how to find us. But the eight-year-old big mouth obviously didn't understand that.

"We live in Trojan Pines," Cassie announced.

"Oh, y'all rich black kids," Snake snapped, looking down on us. "Guess we better leave y'all alone. Or maybe messing with you will be extra fun."

The short guy yelled from behind me, "Go on an' let 'em pass, Snake."

Snake gave his friends an evil eye. He hesitated a second, then looked back at my brother. "Looks like it's your day. My boy Rock thinks I ought to let y'all through." Snake grabbed Clay's collar. "Don't let me catch you on this path again. And I was just testin' you about smokin'. You passed! Now get on outta here."

I wanted to tell those boys that if they stopped smokin' bad stuff, maybe they could have a better life. And the name Snake was yucky. However, I was smart and kept my comments to myself, just praying things would turn around for them.

The three of us ran all the way home. We were so happy to see the two-story redbrick building. Once safely in the driveway, we made a pact not to mention this to our parents. We were scared we might get in trouble with our parents, and those dudes, if we blabbed.

Unfortunately, when we got to the door, our mother was waiting with a not-so-happy look on her face. When we confessed to her what happened, she was especially disappointed with Clay because he was the oldest and should have been more responsible. However, she praised him for taking responsibility by admitting that taking the shortcut was his idea. Even though I couldn't wait to get older, it's not so fun taking all the weight sometimes.

✪

That next week the three of us became homebodies again. Our one adventure outside the neighborhood was enough excitement to last for a while.

At church on Sunday, my mother met our neighbor whose home had been badly damaged by the storm. They were living in a hotel until their place was fixed. Mrs. Anderson and my mom learned they had a lot in common. Both had a son and two daughters, all of us about the same ages. Mom invited them over for dinner and fellowship that evening so we could do something loving for a family in need.

Mom had the house spotless, and it smelled better than a bakery in the early morning. All the packing boxes were put away, and everything was in its place. For the first time, our house felt like a home. When the Andersons arrived, our family was excited.

Mrs. Anderson's older daughter was a shy girl named Riana. Her skin was the color of the sand on the beaches. Instantly, I loved her long, straight hair. My hair wasn't short, but hers had mine beat. We were about the same height, and I wondered if we could be friends. I showed her to my room. The two of us just sat there, quiet as mice nibbling on cheese.

Cassie and Riana's little sister, Rolanda, were running up and down the stairs, apparently pretending their Barbie dolls were flying in a helicopter. Clay and his new best buddy, KJ, short for Kevin Jr., were playing computer games. My dad and Mr. Anderson talked about the up-coming football season for the Trojans, where my dad would be coaching.

"Are you going into the fifth grade too?" Riana asked me.

"Yep," I answered.

"I can introduce you to lots of people at school. You won't have to worry about being the new kid on the block. Since you have me as a friend, you'll have plenty of pals. Before you know it, you won't even miss your old friends."

Riana knew nothing about my old friends or me. Even though she was trying to help me adjust, there was no way I could ever forget my best friend, Jillian.

"Friends mean a lot to me," I said. "Not everyone knows how to be a true friend."

"I know you were probably tight with someone at your old school. Finding somebody to take that place won't be easy. But we just left church. Where's your faith?"

Even if I could replace Jillian, I wasn't sure I wanted to.

"Give me a shot at being your buddy," Riana urged me. "You know, whenever I'm a little afraid to take a risk, my mom says I'm like a baby bird that's never flown. Until it leaves the tree and spreads its wings, that little bird will never know it can fly."

Even though her words made sense, I wasn't ready to let a new friend in. Besides, the experience with Snake and his crew was bothering me. And I was still shaken up by last week's storms. All those things added together really scared me. Trying to get through it all was all I could do to make it past dinner.

✪

After I said my prayers that night, Mom came into my room. She sat on the bed and gently placed my head in her lap. Braiding my hair, she said, "Baby, I know there's something wrong. If you want to share it, I'm all ears. Maybe I can make whatever isn't right better."

"Why hasn't Jillian called me?" I asked my mom. "I've been gone for two weeks, and I've left her two messages."

Mom said, "Just give her a chance; maybe she's just busy, honey."

Next, I told my mom how afraid I was of storms. "When the rain comes, I get frightened. What if the hail messes stuff up or the lightning starts a fire?" I started to shake. Tears fell down my face, but I felt comfort in my mother's arms.

After kissing me on the forehead, she uttered softly, "Second Timothy 1:7 says, 'For God hath not given us the spirit of fear; but of power, and of love, and of a sound mind.' Carmen, I don't know what tomorrow holds either. I get afraid sometimes too. But I believe the Lord holds our future. He loves us. Next time you feel afraid, just recite that Scripture. Though you can't see God, He's there. Then you can face the future with a smile. I call that stepping out happily on blind faith."

3
Noticing Differences

By the end of August, I was finally begin-ning to settle into my new environ-ment. But I still felt uneasy. All my life I'd lived in a mostly white area. This was going to take some getting used to.

Lots of people from church, the neighbor-hood, and the university had us over for dinner.

One Sunday after worship service we were invited to our new pastor's home for a congregation potluck. Reverend and Mrs. Wright's children were away at college, but there were a lot of other kids there. The adults ate under the shade trees.

I played kickball with my brother, sister, and a bunch of other kids from church we'd never met.

When the other team kept putting their best kicker up to bring the loaded base runners home, I yelled with one hand on my hip, "You all can't play that way."

One girl, who was as tall as my brother and looked tough, said I talked funny.

Darren, a boy Clay had told me was in the sixth grade, said, "Naw, she don't sound funny. She just sounds like a white girl."

"What?" I replied in anger. "I don't even want to play with you guys."

"Yep, yep, whatever you say, Miss Goody Two-shoes," Darren teased.

"For your information, I don't think I'm better than anyone else," I said before heading over to my folks. "I'm just me . . . Carmen Lynn Browne. If you don't like the way I talk, then get out of my face. I never asked you to talk to me anyway."

Darren smiled. My tough words didn't seem to affect him at all.

Darren rushed up to me and tried to give me a high five. "Well, at least you got attitude like a sista." He took off and started bullying some other kids when I turned and walked away from him, and the game broke up.

What Darren said bothered me for the rest of the night, while I tried to relax at home. Did I really sound white? And if I did, was that so awful? What did that mean, anyway?

✪

Riana came over to my house while her parents met with the man fixing the storm damage to their home. We sat out in the front yard because Riana wanted to watch her house being fixed.

"I'm so happy God is making our home look better than before," she said.

I was happy too, because it looked like the Lord was making something good come from something bad. Switching the subject, I told her about Darren. To my surprise, she told me that Darren lived down the street. I had no idea he was so close. The thought of running into him all the time made my stomach drop.

"Oh, don't worry about him," Riana said with confidence. "He's real cool." She giggled. "Every time I see him, he asks if I'm 'keepin' it real.'

"Darren acts all smart, but he's not really. He's supposed to be in the seventh grade. But two years ago he failed fourth grade. So now he's in sixth."

Maybe if Darren used correct English, I thought, *he'd do better in school.* I wondered why people gave this guy so much respect and hushed up every time he talked.

"It's getting hot out here," Riana said. "Let's go inside and get some cold lemonade."

We went inside and washed up. Afterward, we placed

our cold glasses half full of lemonade on the table and sat down for some girl talk.

"It really bothered you when Darren said you sounded white, huh?" Riana said, reaching for her drink and then sipped it down.

It really did bother me, but for some reason I wasn't ready to tell Riana everything I was feeling. So I shrugged my shoulders instead, as my body said what my mouth couldn't.

Riana got up and poured herself some more. "Why do you care what he thinks?"

I'd been asking myself that all day. The harder I tried to shake his comments, the more his cruel words got under my skin.

"Being the only black girl in my class for years, I've had to be tough. People always made rude comments about my dark skin. I guess I just figured that being around more black people would make my life easier. I hoped I would be accepted because I looked like everyone else. But Darren reminded me that I'm still different, and I admit that does bother me."

Riana gulped down her last drop of her second glass of lemonade. "Everybody gets picked on for something. We're all different. Either you're too tall, too short, too dark, too fat, too skinny, too smart, or too dumb."

What a cruel world, I thought. I wondered what my "too" category would be that year.

"I'm glad we're friends," Riana said. "I finally have a buddy who likes me for me."

"Yes, you do," I agreed as we gave each other a quick hug.

✪

I'd been looking forward to going school shopping all summer long. My mom, brother, sister, and I, got up early Saturday morning to go shopping. We wanted to be there as soon as the stores opened. My father was at work getting ready for the football team's first game of the season. But the rest of the family piled into our car and headed to the mall.

As we were driving, I thought about Jillian.

"Mom, do you remember last summer when I went to Jillian's slumber party?"

She nodded. That horrible experience had made me feel so unwanted. I left the party early and raced home in tears.

"Remember Jillian's cousin from Seattle, who said she wouldn't spend the night if a black girl was sleeping over?"

"Yes," Mom responded. "Remember, Carmen, like your dad and I have explained to you before, that's called prejudice. Some people don't want to be around you because you aren't like they are; they judge people from the outside. Then sometimes they say or do ugly things."

Mom explained to me as we approached the mall that prejudice is even found in corporations that own stores where we shop. She said some corporations had special programs to help minorities get into business and succeed. "Hopefully," she said, "that will make it possible for more minority-owned stores to be built in the future. It's not all the white people's fault," she said, almost to herself. "A lot of minority stores don't get support."

"Why?" I asked, not really understanding.

"Lots of reasons. But some that come to mind are because the customer service isn't always good, or because the prices may be higher, or because some blacks would rather spend their money at a white-owned store. They sometimes think the black person's items aren't as good."

How crazy is that? I thought. I was glad I judged people for who they were and not by what they looked like.

"Thanks to affirmative action," Mom said, slightly pinching my chin, "things are changing for the better. Maybe when you're an adult, the world will be more balanced."

I didn't fully understand the meaning of *affirmative action*. But I didn't ask Mom to explain further, because I was ready to get a brand-new wardrobe. The prejudice issues would have to be picked up another day, because right now, it was shopping time!

✪

This black college football-game thing was a new experience for me. The crowd was more into the cheerleaders groovin', the dancers twistin', and the band jammin' than they were into the team playin'. I must admit those three groups did spark excitement. I was used to hearing stiff bands play fight songs during all four quarters. Not these guys. These Trojans were jammin' to the latest hits.

Clay was allowed to stand on the field with Dad. I sometimes wished I could be down near the pretty cheerleaders. But no, Cassie and I had to sit up in the press box with our mom. I always hated that place, because you couldn't say a word once the game got started. The kids had to just sit there, eyes glued to the field. But all the adults, who my mom said were educators, trustees, and alumni, were talking to one another the entire game. It was basically one big party. They did watch the team a little. But that wasn't their first priority.

"Where are the TV cameras?" Cassie asked.

We were used to seeing sportscasters every week. My sister loved watching the sports shows, because she wanted to be like people on the TV. Because she was only eight years old, I figured she'd probably change her mind a million times. However, I had to give it to her—Cassie was serious about her little dream. She was always talking to the television crews, asking lots of questions about how everything worked. But no major network was shooting this event. Not even Black Entertainment Television. That was a bummer, because Dad had told me that colleges earn a lot of money from TV appearances.

"This is a smaller school," I explained to my sister, "so I don't think they're on TV every week. Maybe next week."

I looked for my mother and found her at the refreshment table speaking with an older gray-haired gentleman with a full beard. Standing beside him was the cutest boy I'd ever seen. His face was round, and he had dimples in his cheek. He had an afro with naturally curly hair. He wasn't as tall as Clay, but he was tall. And his teeth were white and straight. Yep, he was cute.

When the man saw me staring, I turned away. But he walked toward us, the boy following him.

"Hello, girls," the man said. "I'm President Webb. I have the honor of running this university. This is my grandson, William Spencer Webb III."

"They call me Spence," the boy said. He wore a navy blue and orange Virginia State T-shirt and jeans.

President Webb told us that his grandson attended Ettrick Elementary. He was going into the fifth grade.

"I'm very excited to have your father on our coaching staff this year," President Webb said. "Our football program can sure use his experience. Those boys of ours need good role models and strong discipline."

I smiled when he shook my hand, and then he sat down at the front of the box. His grandson stayed near the food table and loaded up his plate. Boy, was he greedy! He stacked his plate with three hot dogs, two large pieces of fried chicken, corn on the cob, and a bunch of baked beans.

During halftime, Cassie found a girl her age to hang out with. My mother was busy socializing with the other coaches' wives. I was bored. Part of me wanted to chat with Spence. But I didn't know what I'd say to him, so I sat down and placed my chin in the palm of my hands. As I was watching the people walk past the box below me, my mom came over to me. "You don't look like you're enjoying yourself."

I shrugged.

"You still want to go downstairs and buy a T-shirt?"

I looked up at her. "Can I?"

"If you come right back." She handed me twenty dollars. "Yes, I want my change," she said as I smiled slyly, wanting to spend all the money.

On the way to the clothes booth, I ran into a rally of some kind. A guy was standing on a platform, calling for attention. He was clutching a clipboard.

"Ever since the state of California voted to get rid of affirmative action, other states across this nation have been searching for ways to dismantle it too," the guy with the microphone said. "Signing this petition will let the politicians and legislators in Richmond know that we still want it, that we still need it, and that we care about our future. And that the only way we'll get equal opportunity is to keep affirmative action alive."

It was hard to get through the crowd, because a lot of adults and college kids were listening to the guy. He seemed pretty firm with his presentation. Caring about people's hearts was important to me. I believed that as long as a person was good at heart they should get good things in life. Maybe my way of thinking was too far out.

As I finally slid by the crowd and walked toward the clothes booth, I remembered something my dad's mother, Grandma Anna Belle, told me once. She said that black folks aren't where we used to be, but we still weren't where we needed to be. The short time I'd spent in this new town had helped me understand her point.

I wished things were more equal in the world. I didn't know how that could happen. But I decided to pray and learn as much as I could. Yeah, the Lord would have the answers.

"Whatever needs to happen," I mumbled to myself, "I hope it happens soon. I'm tired of noticing differences."

4

First Glance

"You can't judge a book by its cover," my dad said as we drove home from the game.

"What do you mean?" Cassie asked.

"When I first took this job, I heard a lot of negative things about the football team. I was told the guys were lazy and unmotivated. My faith allowed me to cast all the doubt away. I believe in these guys."

Dad told us that winning the game let him know what his players could achieve. "Most people have more to them than what you see," he said. "If we see something bad in a friend, it might be our job to pull out the good in that person."

"What does that have to do with book covers?" I asked.

He chuckled. "You've got to spend time reading a book to truly know what it's all about, Miss Lady. Books are like people in that you can't size them up before you take time getting into all the parts. You guys remember that as you make new friends. Don't judge them by what you see. Get deeper and become friends with kids who believe in God and have good hearts."

"Then if I get a friend like that, Daddy," Cassie asked, "will we get along all the time?"

Dad laughed. "I wish I could say yes for sure, sweetie pie, but you'll still probably have slight differences. Just having friends that love God like you do helps to minimize the . . . drama, as you guys call it."

"Go, Dad," I teased.

He smiled.

★

That night in bed, I thought about my dad's statements. I'd been excited about the fifth grade. Now I was scared. Would the kids in my class like me? Would I get along with them? Could I continue to get good grades? Would I like the school activities? Unfortunately, I had no answers. But I did know that I couldn't judge what my school was going to be like until I went there.

I tossed and turned all night.

Before I knew it, Mom was waking me up for Sunday church service. I rolled over and tried to go back to sleep. But my mother's serious tone told me my idea was not an option.

At the breakfast table Clay said to Daddy, "That game yesterday was awesome. Beating the Tigers by twenty points was so cool."

Dad patted my brother on the back. "You'll be ready for the high school team soon. You're already in seventh grade. Time to take your playing up to another level. I hear the athletic program at the middle school is great. Having you on their team will only make them greater."

"Pops, you know I don't want to play football any-more," Clay said with distress in his voice.

"Ah, Son," my dad responded, "that's just nerves talk-ing. Sure, there will be bigger, tougher, and faster boys on the field this year, but don't you worry. I plan to have you ready. You'll be all right."

I caught a peek of Clay's face, and I knew he wouldn't be all right. He truly did not want to play football. He didn't want to be involved with any sport. And that wasn't because he was lacking in the talent department. My brother could play ball. But Clay would rather spend his time playing on his computer than playing sports . . . unless he was playing a sports-themed video game.

✪

"Y'all got some change to spare?" the homeless man asked as people strolled by him and entered the Zion Hill Baptist Church.

Dirt covered the dark man's face. He smelled like he didn't have a clue what a bath was. His T-shirt, which was obviously once white, was stained with every color of the rainbow. Holes covered his tennis shoes. Although I felt sad for him, I was afraid of how rough he looked.

About thirty people went into the church doors before my family. Not one stopped to give the man change. I didn't think we were going to either. However, when the man stared eye-to-eye with my father and asked for money, Dad gave him a ten-dollar bill.

"Do you really think he's gonna use it for a good cause?" Clay questioned. "I saw on the news that some street beggars take money from hardworking people and then use it to buy alcohol or drugs."

My dad stopped just before we entered the front door of the church. "Remember what I said to you yesterday about prejudging people?"

My brother nodded.

"How can we know this man won't use the money wisely? Something really tragic could have happened to put him in that situation. We never know when we might need someone's help. We should always think twice before we make judgments about someone's situation."

Zion Hill was similar to my old church, Mount Calvary Baptist Church. Though we lived in a white area, my family drove thirty miles to the nearest black church. Now our drive wasn't that far. We only had to ride ten minutes over to Petersburg, Virginia.

The pastor caught my attention as he spoke boldly. "I went to a play last week. Actually, my wife dragged me to it. It was a Christian musical. Don't tell her, but I actually enjoyed it."

The congregation chuckled. I hoped I'd get to go to a play soon. I loved musicals.

"In the front of that theater," the reverend continued, "sat a smelly, dirty man. He was asking folks dressed in their evening best for money. Hardly anyone gave him anything. After the play started, we found out that the man was a member of the cast. He was playing the part of Jesus in the production. I was so moved by that, I asked Deacon Ray to do the same thing for me." He paused as people in the congregation shook their heads and stared at the floor. "Some of you are probably feeling bad about passing by that homeless man this morning."

Wow, I thought to myself. *The man out front was acting. But he looked so real. He wasn't Jesus, but he could have been.*

"Some of you walked right past him. You only took into account what you saw. You didn't tell him about the love of God or take a moment to pray for him," Reverend Wright admonished us. "I saw most of the congregation walk by without giving a penny. I'm often tempted to ignore people begging due to my uncertainty of their character. But God doesn't ask us to judge others, or to determine if they are worthy of our charity. He just wants us to give and pray."

Reverend Wright then told Deacon Ray to stand and give a report of the money collected. When a low number was announced, the crowd grew loud, and I saw lots of people shaking their heads. Then our pastor accepted the large, practically empty basket from Deacon Ray and told us that the collected funds would be donated to a homeless shelter.

"This message is for you kids too," the pastor added, walking into the congregation. "As you enter another school year tomorrow, try being a better person than you were last year. Try loving your neighbors. Try being your brother's keeper. Try not judging people. Be better than some of us adults, who are set in our ways. We're often scared to go out on a limb and trust people." He stopped in the aisle beside me. "I'm not saying you won't get hurt along the way. I'm not saying trust strangers. But if you keep God in your heart, He will always protect you."

✪

"We're in the same class; isn't that great?" Riana announced as she saw both of our names posted on the same class list in the gym. Our teacher's name was Miss Pryor.

"How cool!" I was glad I'd have at least one buddy in the class.

Back in July, Mom had taken my little sister and me for a tour of the school building. But the place looked different with people in it. Rolanda, Riana's sister, knew her way around. Although she and Cassie wouldn't be in the same class, she promised to take my sister to her new room.

"Come on—let's get a good seat," Riana said with excitement as she pulled me up the stairs. "We're fifth graders, so we're the oldest. We get to run this place."

At my old school, elementary wasn't finished until the sixth grade. Here at Ettrick, the fifth graders were the cream of the crop. I had waited so long to be in the oldest grade. Maybe getting that wish a year early was compensation for having to move.

When we arrived at room 202, we found lots of classmates already at the desks. We couldn't find any two seats together up front. However, we walked across the front aisle looking at the back rows.

I stopped my feet from moving another inch when I saw Spence Webb, the cute boy from the football game, standing near a seat in the back. I hadn't had a chance to tell Riana about him.

To my surprise, I caught her staring in Spence's direction. My friend grabbed my shoulder and whispered, "I can't believe he's in our class!"

I didn't want to have a crush on the same guy my friend liked. But Spence was cute. His gingerbread complexion and teddy bear smile made him absolutely adorable.

"That's a cute black shirt he has on," Riana said with a sigh.

I blinked. Spence wasn't wearing a black shirt. But the guy standing next to him was.

I sighed with relief. "I thought you were talking about Spence."

Riana turned quickly to me. "How do you know Spence?"

"I met him Saturday at Virginia State's football game," I said.

Riana nodded. "His grandpa does something impor- tant over there, doesn't he?"

"Dr. Webb is the president of the university. I'd say that's pretty important," I joked. "Spence and I didn't talk a lot, but he seemed nice," I said, trying not to look at him.

I'd never liked a boy before. I hadn't been sure I liked Spence until I thought my friend liked him.

"What's the name of the guy in the black shirt?" I asked.

"That's Hunter Jones," Riana told me with a big smile. "He was in my class last year. We were science partners. I really missed Hunter over the summer. I think that means I like him. I'm glad he's in my class again anyway."

Riana asked people to move so we could sit together, but no one would budge. We ended up taking two seats in the second-to-last row. In my old school, I usually sat in the front row. The board was so clear from there.

Riana pulled out her reading glasses and put them on. She didn't seem to mind the distance. I didn't either when I noticed Spence and Hunter take the seats right behind us. The boys said hello as they sat down. My friend and I just giggled.

Mrs. Morgan, the principal, came on the loudspeaker. As she gave a welcome and the announcements, I checked out my new surroundings. Three bulletin boards were up at the front of the class. One had the words *math* and *science* in bright red cut-out letters. *Reading* and *English* were placed in blue on the other board. The third bulletin board behind Miss Pryor's desk was blank.

There were thirty seats in the room, five rows with six desks in each. Every place was filled but one. That made twenty-nine students in the class.

Just then, the door opened, and a girl rushed in. She was shorter than me with dark chocolate skin and short hair.

After she spoke to the teacher, the girl took the last empty seat in front of Spence. She looked around the room and made eye contact with Spence and Hunter.

Riana leaned over and nodded toward the girl. "That's Layah Golf," my friend whispered. "She's the best athlete at this school. All the guys like to hang with her. They think she's cool. I think she's a tomboy."

That skinny little thing, an athlete? I thought. She looked like she'd tip over if she held my CD player in her hand.

"She plays football, volleyball, basketball, soccer, softball, kickball, tennis . . . everything but the sport like her name, golf." Riana snorted.

Miss Pryor called the class to order. She started with an overview of what we could expect from the year. She announced that this was an advanced class and that she'd be expecting a lot out of us. I must have done well on my placement test to land with this smart group. When I saw some other surprised faces, I realized I wasn't the only one who was not aware that this was an accelerated fifth grade class. My parents would be pleased.

Miss Pryor seemed really nice. She was young and pretty. This was her first year at the school. Just like me.

✪

Lunchtime was the first break of our long morning. Miss Pryor pointed out three big tables that were set aside for our class. We could sit anywhere at those tables, she said, after we received our food. But if we caused too much trouble sitting where we wanted, she would assign seats.

Hunter and Spence stood in line behind Riana and me. When Riana asked me how I liked the new school, I told her it had definite potential. She grinned, catching my hint about the cute boys behind us.

When we had our food, Riana found four seats together. We hoped Hunter and Spence would take the other two.

As the boys started toward us, my heart skipped a beat.

Just before they reached our table, Layah walked up to them.

"Oh, Hunter, don't sit there," she said smoothly. "You and Spence come over here, and let's rap."

"That's a bet," Hunter agreed as he followed Layah.

Spence looked at Riana and me and shrugged. "See you after lunch," he said before joining his friend.

We watched the guys move away from our table. But before they sat down, a fight broke out. A big girl tripped Layah. Then she started beating up on the girl, who probably was double her weight.

Some people cheered. I couldn't understand how anyone could applaud someone else's pain. The whole thing scared me. I'd never witnessed girls fight. I'd only seen them argue. Layah must have felt she was right because the other girl started the fight. But in my mind there was no reason for what she was doing.

We hadn't been in school a whole day, and I had already learned a great lesson. It was like my dad said after the game. And Reverend Wright said at church. I hadn't truly understood the meaning of prejudgment until that moment. Although I didn't really know Layah, she seemed like a pushover in the classroom. But I knew now she was nothing like what I had seen at first glance.

5
Cloudy View

Marble-sized hail filled the streets as I glanced out the classroom window that Friday afternoon. Thirty minutes were left until the first week of school was over. For the most part it had been a great one, but today my emotions mirrored the gloomy outdoors.

Layah had been out Tuesday, Wednesday, and Thursday because she was suspended for fighting on the first day. Since no one had talked to her, there was still no explanation for what happened. I didn't think about her while she was absent. My time was filled with making and enjoying new friends. Riana introduced me to the people she had known for years.

Thursday was especially fun. Miss Pryor asked us to break into groups of four and solve twenty math word problems. Hunter and Spence asked Riana and me to work with them. We had a great time, not just doing the work, but telling a few jokes on the side.

We worked so well as a foursome that we finished early. Our teacher said that as long as we kept the noise down, we could remain huddled. With the free time, we talked about our families.

I learned Spence was an only child. "I used to want a sibling," he said. "Now I've decided I like all the attention."

I teased him, claiming he was more spoiled than year-old milk. Laughingly, he agreed!

Hunter said his parents had divorced a few years ago. He and his two older twin sisters, Hayli and Haven, lived with their mother. They were in the seventh grade.

When Miss Pryor dismissed the class, Hunter said, "I think the four of us worked so well together, we should stay a team like this all year."

"Great idea," Riana replied. "You guys would never have finished early without Carmen and me."

We all left the classroom laughing.

When I got up on that dreary Friday morning, Riana called to ask if I'd collect her assignments that day. Her family was finally moving back into their home from the hotel.

The thought of having my new close friend three doors down the block was extra cool. Even though I was making other friends in room 202, no one made me feel as comfortable as Riana.

"I'll miss you today," I told Riana.

"I'll miss you too," she said.

Just as I hung up the phone, I heard thunder. As I peeked out the window, I could see nothing but darkness.

✪

On Layah's first day back to school, not a soul dared ask her about the fight. The mean look she wore said she didn't plan on discussing the incident.

Friday was gym day for all fifth graders. We met our PE teacher, Mr. Dubois, in the gym. He was tall with skin that looked like caramel and reminded me of what Spence could maybe look like twenty years from now. With the rain still falling, there was no way we could play outside. While the class warmed up for indoor volleyball, I noticed Miss Pryor smiling and laughing with the handsome Mr. Dubois.

Mr. Dubois chose two captains. One was Layah. The other was Sammy Morgan, a large fellow, frowning and wearing his shirt hanging out of his pants.

"I don't care who you pick, Sammy," Layah bragged. "Any team you put together can't beat mine."

"Oh, talk trash now," Sammy defended himself, "'cause when we clean up, you'll be eating those words."

My skills at volleyball weren't that sharp. But no one

at this school would know that. Still, neither Layah nor Sammy chose me. When I remained standing alone after everyone else had been picked, I realized there was already an even number of students on each team. Riana's absence had made the count uneven.

I overheard Hunter and Spence ask Layah to pick me.

"No way," she said. "I don't like her, so she's not going to play on my team. I don't see why you two think she's cool."

Mr. Dubois didn't seem to hear them. "You can keep score, Carmen," he suggested.

From that moment on, no one in the class talked to me. At lunch, I sat alone, like a person on a deserted island. Although I put up a tough front, my heart was breaking. What did I do wrong? Last time I checked, I didn't have the cooties. My hopes for a great school year seemed to fade along with my hopes for afternoon sunshine.

★

"We'll straighten all this out on Monday," Riana uttered with confidence while we cleaned up her room that Friday evening. Because no one talked to me after gym class, I felt really alone. Riana was not even in school, but as soon as I exited off the bus, I zoomed to her house. I wanted to make sure she wasn't mad at me too. Fortunately, I found her to be the same old, fun-loving Riana.

There was one difference, however. My usually tidy

friend had boxes everywhere. To swiftly straighten her room, we asked our mothers if I could spend the night to help her. They both thought it was a wonderful idea.

"It's not you. I bet Layah has the problem and just took it out on you. And then . . . whatever she says . . . however she feels . . . well, the rest of the people follow along as if she has them tied to a string, like puppets," Riana rationalized.

"That's not fair! That's not right. Everyone liked me all week. Why would they let her turn them against me? Most of the week she wasn't there. How can Layah not like me? I don't understand. I'm really glad you'll be back in school on Monday. I know that might not make the class treat me better, but . . . at least I will have you as a friend."

Riana sat next to me on the edge of her canopy bed, placed her arm securely around my shoulder, and said, "You're right! No matter how they act, you'll always have me as a friend."

✪

"What do you mean, you aren't going to football practice?" my father bellowed from the kitchen as I walked into our house Saturday morning.

I wondered what the yelling was about. Then the answer popped into my brain like a popcorn kernel. Even without hearing the other part of the conversation, I realized my dad and my brother were disagreeing over Clay's spot on the team.

Clay had given middle-school football a shot for our father's sake. But he told me on Wednesday that he'd quit the team. Even though he had peace, he was wrestling with how his decision would affect our dad.

"With all the talent you've got," Dad said firmly, "you're letting football go?"

Clay didn't back down from what he felt. "That's just it. I'm not naturally talented like you. I have to work harder than the other guys to keep up. I have to give every play everything I got. Nothing on the field is easy for me. And I don't like it."

Although I couldn't see my brother's face, his voice told me he had a face full of anger. I understood both sides. Dad had always wanted Clay to be a jock. Clay had always wanted to succeed in anything other than sports.

"I promised I'd try it," Clay said, "but I don't like it."

Clay left the kitchen and headed downstairs. He hustled past me at the front door.

Dad followed down after him and grabbed his shirt. "Don't walk away from me. We're not finished with this conversation. You're going to school today, and you are gonna play."

"Be real about it," Clay said, tugging away from Dad's grip. "I'm not you. I'm not even your real son anyway."

My dad looked deflated by those words as he watched Clay head downstairs. I was in shock. What had my brother just said? Surely he had to be joking. But why would he say it?

Clay had been with us for as long as I could remember. I did notice that there were no baby pictures of him in the house. The walls were occupied with tons of baby photos of Cassie and me. It never crossed my mind to ask about it. From age four to twelve, Clay's mug was plastered in more places than I cared to look at.

Picking up my overnight bag, I stood there, stunned.

Dad didn't say a word. I could tell by the sad look on his face he was torn up by Clay's words. For a long second he stared at the downstairs steps. He uttered, "No, I need to calm down. I'll speak to him later." He then headed upstairs.

As I went to my bedroom, I was deep in thought. If Clay was adopted, maybe I was too. Maybe all three of us weren't being raised by our birth parents.

The thought of us not being a real family scared me. I worried that our other parents could come anytime and take us away. Or worse, that Mr. and Mrs. Browne might have stolen us. I wondered who would raise us if they got caught and went to jail. The people I knew as my parents had never told me I was adopted, but they had never said I wasn't either.

Was everything I'd known all my life one big lie? The only way I could find out was to speak with Mom, but she wasn't around. She was in her bedroom calming my father down before he left for Virginia State's second home game.

Unable to control my weird thoughts, I prayed, *Dear God, the last couple of days have been pretty tough. I can't really see anything in my future. I need You to show me the light. I need You to step in and brighten my world. I need You to give me answers. Help me, Lord. Help me. Amen.*

✪

Dad got home late Saturday night because the game was delayed due to rain. When he arrived he was in a decent mood. A lot better than when he left. The Trojans had won again. The margin of victory was even better. They beat Hampton University by twenty-seven points.

Clay had kept himself locked in his room for a while, as if he were a prisoner. He didn't even come out for lunch. Cassie and I wanted to talk to him, but Mom ordered us to leave him be.

I tried to discuss the adoption business with my mother that afternoon. She stared at me with a sparkling tear in her dark brown eyes and said we'd talk about everything when my dad got home. After hearing that, like Clay, I confined myself to my room. Since the rain continued to pour, I couldn't go outside to think.

Cassie came into my room to bother me, since she was banned from bugging Clay. Right off the bat, she knew I wasn't up to playing games. Of course, she asked what was wrong, but I couldn't bring myself to tell her. My little sister did not need to join in carrying the burden that was wearing me down. I told her to get out and leave me alone. Then I felt bad afterward.

"Kids," Dad yelled throughout the house about ten o'clock that night. "Y'all come on in the kitchen. We need to have a family discussion."

We all assembled around the kitchen table. Mom had chocolate milk on the table and chocolate chip cookies in the oven. I figured if we were getting snacks late at night, something was wrong.

"I don't know where to start," my mother said with a sigh, her head down.

My dad caressed her back. "Just speak from your heart. Tell the kids what you feel."

Taking a deep breath, my mom said, "When your father and I got married years ago, the first thing we talked about was starting a family one day. We both wanted children, but we thought it best to wait awhile and get adjusted to each other. One day the time felt right. So we tried to have a baby. After two years of trying, there was no success. We were so troubled."

My mother told us that, during that period of time, they started meeting couples who had adopted children. In those encounters, they learned how wonderful adoption could be for both the child and the parents. However, at the time, they decided to set adoption aside and visit a fertility clinic, a place that helps people get pregnant.

After one month of going to the doctor, my parents got pregnant with me. I was relieved to know I wasn't adopted. But after hearing my mother speak, I decided it wouldn't have been so bad if I were.

Two years after me, they found themselves blessed with an unexpected child. That's when Cassie came along.

Physically, my mother could have had more children. However, she and Dad had a stronger desire to adopt. They learned the greatest need at most agencies was for parents to adopt African-American boys. Since they had two girls, my parents thought that having a son would make the family complete. Working with the state, the caseworker, and the adoption agency, Clay came to the Browne household at the age of four.

"Son," our father said, "I was wrong to push you so hard about football. I'm sorry I wanted my life to be yours. I love you for who you are. And I'm proud of who you're turning out to be . . . even without sports."

Daddy hugged Clay tighter than I'd ever seen them embrace. I had been worried all day that they would never get along again. My heart felt lighter as I witnessed the two of them bonding.

"Girls," my father said as he turned to Cassie and me, "I love you both too. We are all one family. It doesn't matter how the good Lord brought you to us. What counts is that each of you is a special gift from Him. One gift we went and got. One gift we asked for. And one gift was a surprise! All of you are gifts nonetheless. Gifts both your mom and I treasure. As your dad, I won't always be right. But I do want what is best for you. As long as we are a family, we can get through anything."

✪

Although things in my family were better after that, neither the constant rain nor my school situation got better. Riana was back in class on Monday, and that was a good thing. She tried to get people to stop being angry with me. But then Layah turned the class against her too.

"No one wants to be our friend," I blurted to Riana as I picked over my dry hamburger in the lunchroom.

"Oh, Carmen," Riana said, "they'll come around. Right now, they're just seeing through Layah's eyes. For some reason, she has a problem with us. Even though it's wrong, she's passing her feelings on to others. Just as sure as I know the rain will go away, I also know eventually people will like us for who we are. One day we won't be seen through Layah's cloudy view."

6
Hopeful Outlook

"Today is going to be a great day," I encouraged myself as I gazed in the mirror.

It was the beginning of October. Our beautiful state, Virginia, had started changing her appearance. Fall was in full force. I could tell it everywhere I looked.

Riding the bus to school, I observed the gorgeous orange, cranberry, and yellow leaves on the trees. They reminded me that change could be good. However, I was still excited that my best friend, Jillian, was coming to visit in a few weeks.

"See the board behind me?" Miss Pryor pointed out as she talked to us that morning. That board had been empty for a month. Today, it contained the words *affirmative action*.

The teacher told us to write a two-page paper on the subject. It was due December 15, the day before Christmas break.

"Take out a pen and paper," Miss Pryor instructed. "Write across the top of your paper, 'Affirmative Action: Yes or No.'"

The paper was supposed to explain our personal views on the subject. A brief history on the issue was also necessary. I'd always enjoyed writing papers. In previous years, essays had been one of my favorite kinds of assignments. However, in the past I had written on subjects I liked. I remembered my conversation with my mother as we drove to the mall, and she had mentioned affirmative action. So even though my ears had heard the term used several times, I hadn't taken the time to find out what it really was.

Regardless of how I felt about the assignment, it was going to be a big part of my grade. So I had to put aside my feelings and give it my all. Not only were we going to be graded, but our teacher also made it a contest. The bulletin board would hold the papers of first, second, and third places. Those winners would receive As. Special prizes would be given. In addition, the top three papers would be read aloud by the authors at a PTA meeting in January.

Miss Pryor obviously felt this issue was a really big deal. Since it was so important, she thought we should be made aware of something the world had such strong opinions about.

After gathering information about it, she told us, we needed to choose a side and then write about why we chose that side.

At recess time, the beautiful fall day blew nice, warm breezes. The majority of the class played kickball. Riana and I weren't invited to join the game. But it wasn't that big a deal anymore. Sure, I wanted to be accepted. However, my friend and I just focused on what we had—each other.

We weren't the only ones Layah wasn't talking to. She had also cast aside James Taylor, the only white student in our class. James was a math wizard and knew his times tables better than my smart brother. Wendi Bruce was the other outcast. This girl could sing like a sparrow.

A month into the school year, Layah treated the four of us like chicken pox victims.

"So, are you for it or against it?" Riana asked me while throwing pebbles into the pond.

"Please don't laugh," I said, "but I don't really understand what it is."

Riana chuckled.

"I asked you not to laugh."

"I'm not laughing at you," she assured me. "I'm trippin' 'cause I don't know either. My parents think we've got to have it. So I guess that means I'm for it . . . whatever it is."

"You have to know what it means before you can have an opinion," I challenged. "You can't stand on your parents' views forever."

She looked at me like, How'd I know that?

"I heard that from a girl on one of the Disney Channel shows."

"Yeah, I know. Guess I'll find out about it, and then I'll know how I feel."

A red rubber ball rolled up between us. Neither Riana nor I wanted to pick it up. They hadn't picked us, so why should we be nice? Deep down I knew God wanted me to treat people as I wanted to be treated, but my hurt heart made me rebel against doing the right thing. We saw Layah heading our way to retrieve it.

As she snatched the ball from my hands, she said, "Don't you prissy girls wish you were playing? Good thing affirmative action isn't in effect out here on the playground. Nobody is making me pick either of you. You're right where I want you . . . watching. Watching us have all the fun. Watching us make all the moves. Watching us with the power. Yep, you're in your place . . . watching."

If Layah understood the meaning of affirmative action correctly, then I guess I heard her say it was a program that made people with power put people with no power into positions. That made me determined to go to the library and start my research.

If Layah was right, I didn't like affirmative action. I wouldn't need any laws to help me get a job. My brain, talent, and skills would be enough to help me become anything I wanted to be. And if I were ever in a position of power, I would choose from the heart, not because of skin color.

Surely big business executives were fairer at choosing their teams than Layah. They wouldn't keep me out just because they didn't like me. Oh, I hoped that wouldn't be true.

✪

On Saturday night, Rolanda, Riana's sister, had her eighth birthday party. My sister went to the Andersons' to enjoy the festivities. My dad was out of town with the team. My mom was sleeping. So I got busy working on my paper. Clay also stayed home to work on his studies. The house was quieter than a school hall in the summer.

Taking a break, I headed downstairs to visit my brother.

"What are you up to?" I asked Clay after doing a somersault on his empty twin bed.

"Nothing much," he answered. "Just thinking."

"Thinking—with what brain?" I teased my brother. He didn't laugh. "I'm just kidding. What are you thinking about?"

"I don't know if we should discuss what I'm thinking," Clay blurted.

Placing my hand on my hip, I gave him a crazy look. I hoped my stare would make him open up. It didn't.

"No need to shut me out," I pressed. "You're my big brother. We can talk about anything. You always help me out."

"I'm thinking about my other family," he said slowly and softly.

Clay said he felt like it was his fault that his birth parents gave him away. He also wondered if his parents were still alive. Did he have other brothers and sisters? If so, he wondered what they were like. The biggest issue plaguing his heart was whether he should try to find this mysterious family from his past.

He asked for my opinion, but I didn't know what to tell him. I didn't have to walk in his shoes. However, I realized that my world wouldn't be the same without him in it. A selfish part of me didn't want Clay to even think of meeting those other people. If he left to go live with them, I didn't know what that would do to our family. Yet at the same time, I knew he had a right to have his questions answered.

"I don't want you to move away," I told him. "If you did, who'd pick on me?"

"No matter who they are, or where they are, or what they say, I'd never leave you. You're my family."

Those words gave my soul peace. Yet it was clear my brother was still troubled. I looked to heaven for words that could comfort him.

Miraculously, the words came to me. "I'm sure the lady who had you, loved you," I said, "and probably still does. She probably had to give you away. I'm sure she wanted you to have more than she could give you. And

God brought you to Mom and Dad. There's nothing wrong with thinking about your other family."

Clay tried to hide the tears in his eyes. Even though I saw the weak side of him, I didn't say a word. I wanted to encourage him.

"Maybe one day," I continued, "when the time is right, you'll get to meet them. I know they'd be blessed if they spent even one day with you." I socked him gently in the arm. "You need to talk to Mom and Dad about this, though," I said, knowing I'd be praying for him.

"Maybe I will, but don't peep me out on this one."

Pretending to zip my lips, I said, "They're sealed."

✪

Sunday after dinner, my mother told Cassie and me it was time for a tea party. Each of us was allowed to invite two guests to join us for flavored teas, finger sandwiches, and pastries. We gave two tea parties every year: one in the fall and one in the spring.

These parties kept our friendships close but also taught us table manners. We followed the proper rules of etiquette and even dressed up in church clothes.

My sister invited Rolanda and another girl she'd become close to, whose name was Janelle Williams.

I invited Riana, my only friend. I wished Jillian could come, but she lived too far away to come over for only two hours. Besides, she'd be visiting soon and would stay the whole weekend.

Mom gave us each two printed invitations to hand out. "Make sure you deliver them tomorrow," she said, "so your guests can confirm by Wednesday."

Cassie left the room with bundles of energy to place names on her blank envelopes. Mom chuckled as she watched her daughter skip away.

Helping Mom clear the dishes, I moaned, "Do I have to invite two people? Riana is the only friend I have here."

"Why is that?" she asked.

"No one likes me here. And before you ask, I haven't done anything to deserve the cold treatment."

"Are you sure?" Mom probed.

I placed glasses in the sink. "Yes. See, this girl named Layah runs the class. She's decided she doesn't want to have anything to do with me, so no one else will either."

My mother wiped off the counter. "Maybe your second guest should be this Layah girl."

"What?" I shouted as if that was the most absurd idea I'd ever heard. "There is absolutely no way I'd give her an invitation. She'd laugh in my face."

"Don't concern yourself with her response. Be the bigger person. Focus your energy on setting the example. Then even if she laughs, you'll have the satisfaction of knowing you tried. It's always good to treat others as you want to be treated. Make the Lord proud."

I wanted to tell my mother that it would be a cold day

in Florida before I'd reach out to the witch who'd turned the class against me. However, I knew that wasn't the response Mom—or the Lord—wanted to hear. It also wasn't appropriate. Still, being Layah's friend was not in my plans.

"Teas aren't only for socializing with friends," my mother added. "That time can also be used to mend broken relationships. I won't insist that you invite this young lady. That decision is up to you. However, it would be a very nice gesture on your part." She turned off the kitchen lights, and we headed for bed.

Before sliding into my cozy sheets, I filled out my two invitations. One I addressed to Riana, of course. The other pastel purple envelope held Layah's name.

✪

YOU ARE CORDIALLY INVITED TO A
FALL FRIENDSHIP TEA!

Date: Saturday, October 13
Time: 12:00 noon
Place: The Brownes' Tea Room
Attire: Dressy
Theme: Tomorrow will be better with you as my
          friend!
Tea: Whispering Blackberry Currant
RSVP by Wednesday, October 10

✪

"This sounds like so much fun," Riana blurted after reading the invitation that I handed her during class. "I can't wait to come."

"Riana," Miss Pryor scolded, "do I need to move you?" She shook her head.

"The next time anyone talks when I say quiet, I will put the entire class in assigned seats."

I let the rest of the school day pass without delivering Layah's invitation. Seeing her made me rethink my desire to make her a guest in my home. I was afraid she'd hit me if I tried to give her the invitation.

As we left the school building that afternoon, I somehow got up the nerve to say, "Excuse me, Layah." When she turned, I added, "I have something for you."

"What's this?" she asked, grabbing the blackberry-scented envelope from my tight grip.

"It's an invitation to a tea party I'm having this Saturday," I replied quickly. "You don't have to come if you don't want to."

"Me? Go to a tea party? At your house?" Layah laughed. "What makes you think I'd want to go to your party? And why would you want someone there who doesn't like you?"

"I just wanted to invite you," I answered, walking away.

✪

Tuesday Layah ignored me, the same as any other day. I figured she wasn't coming to my tea party since she hadn't said anything about it.

When Wednesday passed and she didn't call, I knew my invitation was declined. Mother was fine with me having only one guest. I was fine too. Just knowing I'd made the effort gave me peace.

✪

Saturday came quickly. I slept in till my mother woke me up at eight.

Mom handed me the cordless phone.

"Hello, Riana," I said, still half asleep.

"It's Layah," said the voice on the phone. "I know it's last minute and all, but my dad said he thought your tea party sounded like a good idea. So if I'm still invited, I'd like to come."

"Sure," I replied in total surprise.

"See you at twelve," Layah said.

Before I could respond, I heard a *click*. I then prayed, *Lord, Layah and I don't get along. Please work a miracle and get her to like me. Amen.*

✪

Guess my prayer worked, because Layah was the nicest she had ever been to me. Seeing her in a dress reminded me of a fish out of water. She only wore boyish-looking clothes every day, very loose-fitting blue jeans and an oversized shirt. Her mannerisms showed that she was very uncomfortable around all this "girlie stuff," so I made every effort to ease the tension.

The ham-and-cheese quiche, salmon finger sandwiches, lemon scones, and miniature cherry cheesecakes were delightful. Topping off the menu was the sweet yet bitter whispering blackberry currant tea. All of us enjoyed a lively conversation. To my surprise, Layah listened more than she contributed.

Riana and her sister had to leave shortly after the food was served to attend an afternoon wedding. I was really worried about entertaining Layah alone.

"I owe you a big apology," Layah said as we sat on the living room sofa with china cups resting in our hands. "You're not half bad. Spence told me your dad is a football coach at State. Maybe I could catch a game with you sometime. I've never had a girlfriend. Most are too prissy. But I could make an exception in your case. When I think of us hangin' in the future, I have a hopeful outlook."

7

Blurred Sight

Is that first number a three or an eight?" I
asked Riana in class as I strained to see
the blackboard Monday morning.

"Do you need my glasses?" she joked.
"That's a six."

The cute red glasses my friend wore en-
abled her to see flies more than twelve feet
away. I didn't need glasses. But I figured I
must have been catching a cold because
things looked kinda fuzzy.

"After you copy all thirty problems, you
may go outside for recess," Miss Pryor
announced.

Riana finished in no time. It took me a
lot longer because I second-guessed everything I saw on the blackboard.

"Do you want me to wait for you?" Riana offered, being a great best friend. "Save our usual spot on the sidelines?"

"No," I said. "You go ahead. I'll catch up with you at the pond."

About ten minutes later, I finally finished. When I looked up, I realized that Layah had finished at the same time. Although we'd had a great talk on Saturday, I didn't know if she'd still act cool toward me.

I was a little scared about going to her. Good thing I didn't have to. She came to me.

"You ready to go outside?" Layah asked when she saw me put my pencil down.

"Yep," I replied.

"We can head out together," she suggested. "I'm going to the bathroom first. Want to walk there with me? I need to tell you something in private."

Layah Golf wanted to walk with me! I was stunned but excited.

I felt pretty important accompanying her to the bathroom. I hadn't realized how happy it would make me to be accepted by her. My heart smiled at the thought of Layah wanting to be my friend.

After washing her hands, she said, "You know, I've been thinking about you and me gettin' tight. There's just one problem."

"Problem?" I repeated.

"Yeah." Her tone became tough. "Your friend Riana is

a problem. I don't like her. If you want to hang out with me, you gotta drop Four-eyes. She just doesn't belong."

Was this bully asking me to dump my friend before she'd accept me?

"Why do I have to choose?" I asked. "Why can't all three of us be friends?"

Layah looked at me as if I'd gotten an F on my spelling test.

"You know, it took me a while to open up to Riana when I first moved here. But I found out that she's really cool! If you gave her a chance, I'm sure you'd like her too."

"Listen," Layah said, staring me eye-to-eye. "I told you, I don't like the girl. That should be enough. Besides, from what I hear, Riana is jealous of you. I'm not one to gossip, but that's what I heard."

I should have pressed Layah for the real reason she didn't like Riana. Maybe it was something that could be fixed. But instead of trying to solve the problem, I simply stared at the beige bathroom wall. Riana, jealous of me? Naw! I started walking out the door.

Before I could leave the restroom, Layah yelled, "If you don't believe me, just see how she acts when I pick you first for the kickball team and she's left standing on the sidelines. See how your so-called friend treats you."

I knew it was wrong to test a friend. I should have ignored Layah's suggestion and simply asked Riana if our relationship was shaky. But I was so drawn to Layah that part of me didn't care what Riana felt.

When Layah and I went outside for gym, she picked me first for her team. I really enjoyed being selected for someone's team. Playing the game was a blast too. My kickball skills were lacking, but Layah didn't seem to mind. She laughed innocently at my mistakes and yelled proudly at my triumphs.

Riana sat alone in our usual spot at the pond.

I could have left the comforts of third base and joined my lonely friend, but I didn't. I could have insisted Layah include her as part of the team, but I didn't. I could have let Riana take my next kick, but I didn't. I didn't share her pain. I didn't stop her pain. And I didn't feel her pain. I just enjoyed my own acceptance. Being a part of the group was a dream I would not allow to be shattered by Riana's sadness. So I played ball and ignored her, like everyone else. What kind of friend was I being to Riana? I didn't care.

"Where's she going?" I heard Layah yell rudely in the middle of our game.

Turning my head to the pond, I noticed Riana sobbing.

"See, Carmen," Layah said, "I told you she's jealous of you. The crybaby can't even stand to watch you have fun. Some friend, huh?"

I belted the ball with anger and frustration. As I ran to home plate, I saw Riana run from the silent pond in tears.

Some friend I was.

✪

Miss Pryor seated us in alphabetical order that afternoon. "Before you complete the problems you copied down, there's something I want to talk to you all about."

Before recess, I'd been in the next-to-last row. After the change, I was seated in the back row. The blackboard was even harder to read.

"The office called during your recess time," she said when we'd settled into our new seats. "One of your classmates came in terribly upset. Apparently some of you have not allowed her to participate in your games. This is totally unacceptable."

I wanted to sink way down in my chair. My friend was in so much pain that she went to the office! I knew deep down it was all my fault.

"From now on, every single person plays, or no one plays. If I find that people aren't being picked, there will be trouble for the whole class." Miss Pryor gave us a look of disappointment. "Tomorrow, recess is canceled."

✪

Two weeks later Jillian, my best friend from Charlottesville, came for a weekend visit. I was in desperate need of a close friend. Riana hadn't spoken to me since I ditched her to hang with Layah. I hadn't exactly tried to reach out to her either. Our friendship was through.

Even though I acted like our breakup was no big deal, I was sad. But Riana seemed to adjust fine. She got to participate in kickball, soccer, track, and every other sport we played at recess. To everyone's surprise, she was a good athlete. Of course, Layah was still the best, but Riana could hold her own. My old friend added flavor and spunk to the other team. They beat us every day. Although I didn't tell her, I was very happy she showed them all what a mistake they'd made by not playing her sooner.

Our mothers encouraged us to work out our differences, but they didn't offer much help in figuring out how.

"So," Jillian asked as we munched on the s'mores we'd made over the crackling fire in my den, "you were telling me about why you guys aren't friends anymore. In your letter you made her sound cool."

Putting down my marshmallow stick, I admitted, "It's my fault."

It was tough to reveal that I'd let a friend down, but Jillian understood.

"You remember Katilyn Callaway, right? The girl we always wanted desperately to hang out with, but she didn't think we were proper enough to be a part of her stuck-up group."

"Yeah, I remember," I said, picturing the girl who always laughed at my outfits.

"I never told you this, but last year she invited me to a sleepover. Katilyn said the only way I could come was not to associate with you anymore." Jillian hung her head. "She told me that black girls and white girls should be cordial to each other, but they should never be close friends. At first, I didn't know what to do. You had always been my friend. But I always wanted Katilyn to be my friend. I felt like you were holding me back from being accepted by the 'in crowd.'"

Laying down her marshmallow stick, Jillian gripped my shoulder. "So I prayed about it, and God helped me see that you had always been there for me. You'd never treated me bad. Katilyn had been mean to me so many times I'd lost count. Why should I leave an awesome friendship for one that was uncertain? So I told Katilyn I didn't want to go to her stuck-up party."

I held my head down. Hearing about her sacrifice let me know what true friendship was all about. It also made me realize that I'd failed Riana. God couldn't be pleased with how I'd responded.

The s'mores lost their appeal. I felt sick to my stomach. For two weeks, I'd been ignoring my good friend. Riana had never treated me badly. She cared for me when no one else in our class did. She had made me laugh when all I wanted to do was frown.

How could I not want Riana in my life? How could Layah give me anything more? The close bond I had lost with Riana had not been replaced by Layah. What had I done?

✪

Jillian and I talked till 1:00 a.m. Then we snuck downstairs to try to watch an R-rated movie on a cable channel. After about three minutes of the film, we were so busy laughing that we didn't notice my mom come in.

"Carmen Browne, you all should be upstairs, number one; and number two, what you're watching is inappropriate. Get upstairs, and I'll deal with you in the morning!"

The next morning, I woke up with Jillian's hand across my face. Her sleeping habits hadn't changed a bit.

I usually slept in on Saturdays, but I didn't want to waste a minute of my precious time with Jillian. I nudged her gently, then poked her until she woke up.

"What?" Jillian yelled, rolling toward me.

"Let's get started," I insisted. "You're leaving first thing tomorrow, and after that who knows when I'll see you again. I've got lots of fun stuff planned for today."

I wondered what my mom was going to say about last night's movie adventure.

After breakfast Mom took us to the mall. Surprisingly, she hadn't chewed me out yet. We had a great time trying on clothes, playing video games, and skimming through bookstores. Jillian and I felt like grown-ups because Mom let us pay for our own lunch in the food court. Jillian had a slice of pepperoni pizza, and I had Chinese food.

After lunch, we caught a movie. Jillian wanted to sit

near the rear. We did at first, but I started squinting. So we moved close to the front to watch the rest of the picture. My mom sat a few rows behind.

"Did you girls enjoy your movie?" my mother asked.

"It was a blast," Jillian and I replied in unison.

"Great, and speaking of movies, last night was an episode that I never want to see again," Mom said. "Both of you know the dangers of watching and listening to inappropriate movies or music. As Christians, we have to be careful about what we allow our eyes to see and our ears to hear."

The two of us knew she was right. Jillian apologized to my mom and said that she'd learned her lesson. I thanked my mom for having mercy on us, because she didn't have to take us to the movies after we'd done wrong.

Jillian was a great friend. Riana and I had been trying to build a friendship like this, before I abruptly and unfairly tore it down.

❂

On Saturday night Jillian noticed papers and books piled high on my desk. She picked up one of the pamphlets. "Affirmative action, huh? What's this for?"

"School project," I answered.

"That's a pretty deep issue," Jillian said.

Since Jillian seemed to know so much about it, I

asked, "What do you think about affirmative action? I mean, who needs a law to help them get ahead? Shouldn't a person's talents be enough?"

"Carmen," she said, "my mom told me that not everyone in this world would judge a person solely for his or her talents. Most employers give people jobs because they like them. And they don't give jobs to people they don't like. Unfortunately, most of the people left out are minority groups. Decision makers generally hire people who are just like themselves—white males."

I wondered if that was why I made the Charlottesville Little Gymnast team the last two years. Over seventy girls had competed for the twelve-member team. Although I was good, the rules required at least one black member and at least one white member to make the team. Both years that I tried out there was only one other black girl competing. She couldn't even do a cartwheel, so I was an automatic selection.

I was beginning to understand why the law was important. But I was still not sure about this whole thing.

Jillian told me that after I moved, things were rough for her. Some kids didn't want to associate with her because she used to hang out with me. Jillian didn't care to hang out with those types of people. However, she did admit that it was hard being alone. Finally, she found people who liked her for what was in her heart. Friends who liked people of all colors. Buddies who had no prejudices.

Jillian said, "Come on, Carmen. Open your eyes and take a look at how bad the world really is. To think things are fair is not really seeing the truth. It's having blurred sight."

8

Optical Nerve

That's why you don't like Riana?" I asked Layah. "Because she wears glasses? That's stupid. And I'm even stupider for following you!"

My head started pounding as I stormed away from Layah. I cut my recess time short and headed back to the classroom.

So many times I had wanted to apologize to Riana, especially when I saw her eating lunch all alone. When she talked with James and Wendi, who both also wore glasses, I wanted to tell her how much I missed our talks. But I never did.

Good thing for me, room 202 was unlocked. I was so upset and disappointed with myself that I didn't bother scanning the room to see if anyone else was using it. I simply headed to my desk in the back row and rested my aching head.

Miss Pryor walked into the room.

"Carmen, what's going on with you?"

"Nothing."

"I know that's not true. Your grades are slipping. When school started you were an A student. Last month you slipped to Bs. I just graded your social studies test, and you got a D. Now, what's wrong?"

"Just stress and pressure, I guess."

Miss Pryor told me that she'd set up a conference with my mother and father. They were going to be so disappointed. "If there's anything I can help you with," she added, "I don't want you to hold back. What's keeping you from being able to focus?"

I didn't know where to begin. So many issues had my stomach tied up in knots. If Miss Pryor knew half of my worries, she'd understand. I had to move and make new friends, and now I was an outcast. I'd just learned about my brother's adoption. And I had betrayed a friend. My head was pounding and throbbing.

Over the next ten minutes she pulled out everything that was inside my soul. She said she'd been wondering why Riana and I weren't talking anymore. Miss Pryor told me she could tell I really missed having Riana as a friend. She said I'd only have peace if I mended my mistake. I knew that was true. But could Riana truly forgive me? After our chat, my head felt better.

I ran outside to get things back on track with my friend. When I arrived at the blacktop, I heard screaming. I busted through a big circle in the crowd and saw Layah. Her back was to me, but I could tell she was talking to someone.

"What's up, yo?" Layah shouted forcefully. "What ya gonna do? Thinkin' ya all that." Since being suspended on the first day of school, Layah had been to the office on three other occasions for picking fights. The principal told her that if she got into trouble one more time, she'd be suspended for ten days instead of three. It appeared Mrs. Morgan's threat didn't matter. Here she was, about to brawl with some poor, innocent soul.

Layah was doing a boxing technique. When she jabbed to the right, I saw Riana standing rigidly in front of her. Without thinking, I quickly stood in front of the friend who had never left my heart. I tried to act like the friend I had never measured up to be.

"Layah, if you want to fight her, you are going to have to fight me too. I am sick of you and this tough-guy stuff. I'm tired of you making people feel they aren't as good as you. I am fed up with you deciding who's in and who's not. Riana has more good qualities than you'll ever have."

A part of me was afraid that my mouth was getting me into trouble that the rest of my body couldn't get me out of. But I didn't back down. I stood firmly planted, like a two-hundred-year-old oak tree. I faced Layah with the courage of a lion.

Even though I probably would not have been able to back up my challenge, Layah must have thought I could. Without a word, she pushed her way through the crowd and left Riana and me alone. Everyone was amazed that she gave up so quickly. Especially me.

I wanted to hug Riana and tell her how sorry I was that I had let her down. But before I got the chance to apologize, Riana said, "Thank you," and left.

She walked with the rest of the class into the building. She wasn't cold and mean, but she wasn't warm and fuzzy either. I couldn't believe I'd expected her to be, when I hadn't been nice to her.

✪

A week later, Thanksgiving break finally arrived. My headaches had gotten more intense. And my relationship with Riana was still strained.

After the incident on the blacktop, I started hanging out alone. I didn't want to hang with Layah, and Riana didn't want me to hang with her. The quiet time helped me make the Lord my best friend. Spending time with Him, I got to see things differently. I used to think friendship was measured by how many friends you had and popularity. Now I knew true friendship should always be measured by quality and sincerity.

Relatives from both sides of our family came up from Durham, North Carolina; but there weren't any kids, just five adults. Since Clay had twin beds, Cassie and I had to bunk with him in his room.

"Pass them string beans," my grandpa Harry said. He was my father's father. He came with his wife, Grandma Anna Belle. Grandma Lula, my mother's mom, came with my mom's sister, Chris, and her husband, Mark. Chris was ten years younger than my mother. Cassie and I loved spending time with her. She was so cool. Auntie Chris and Uncle Mark were almost to their second wedding anniversary. Being a junior bridesmaid in their candlelight Christmas wedding was one of the best experiences of my life.

With our turkey, we had honey-baked ham, barbecued chicken, macaroni and cheese, stuffing, candied yams, mashed potatoes smothered in gravy, collard greens, green bean casserole, corn bread, rolls, fruit salad, banana pudding, apple cobbler à la mode, and red velvet cake. Oh, and my absolute favorite side dish, cranberry sauce. Mixing that slimy red sweet stuff into it made everything on my plate taste good.

"Carmen," Auntie Chris said to me at the table, "your mother tells me you've got a school paper to do on affirmative action. How's it coming?"

"Okay," I said, even though I hadn't started.

"It had better be more than okay," my father said. "Your grades aren't the best, and you need to give every assignment high priority."

I nodded.

"I didn't know you had to write about affirmative action."

"Miss Pryor wants us to give our opinion about it," I said.

"And what is your opinion?" Grandma Lula asked.

I set my fork down, rested my elbows on the table, and twiddled my thumbs. "I'm not really sure."

The whole family questioned me as if I were under arrest. So I said I was more against it than for it. You'd think I'd set off a bomb! Word explosions filled the air as everyone started talking at once.

Eventually, Dad's firm voice got the attention of the floor. "If it weren't for those laws, you wouldn't be where you are today." He stared at me. "If it weren't for affirmative action, your mother and I would never have met, and you would never have been born. You see, your mom and I got into Duke University because of their special admissions program."

Aunt Chris added, "I'm for affirmative action, not just for what it has done for me personally, but for all the good it has done for others. For every black person who doesn't need affirmative action, there are ninety-nine who do."

"Amen to that," Uncle Mark agreed. "Those same anti-discriminatory laws allowed Chris and I to move into our neighborhood in Raleigh."

Grandpa Harry chimed in. "Reverend Martin Luther King Jr., Medgar Evers, and Sister Rosa Parks led the civil rights movement back in the '60s. You weren't born then, but we blacks had it hard in those days. We even had to use different water fountains. What them black leaders did helped us a whole lot. But, baby girl, it still ain't given us no equal playing field. Now, affirmative action won't even the playing field neither. But it will give us minorities a few points on the scoreboard. To win in this-here crazy world, our people need all the help they can get. Not 'cause you and me is special, but 'cause our ancestors gave their lives in hopes that one day we'd have a chance. 'Bout time there were finally some laws to help us get somethin'. Chile, don't think we don't need them laws! We didn't come this far just to start over."

I pondered Grandpa's speech all weekend. Having a wise and loving family gave me plenty to be thankful for. They also gave me plenty of good research for my paper. Maybe I did need to reevaluate my feelings on affirmative action. Could I have been too harsh in my judgment against it?

✪

"I can't need glasses," I whined to the eye doctor as the school nurse handed me a letter to take home to my parents.

The school's annual physical exam checked every student's spine for scoliosis. Our blood pressure was checked, and so was our vision.

"Well, young lady," Dr. Vaughan said, pointing to the chart, "you told me the F was an E. You said the P was a B. Then you thought the G was a C. I'd say you need glasses. You're nearsighted. You can see close up, but you can't see things far away."

At least this explained my headaches. It also told me why I couldn't clearly read the blackboard. Being unable to see the board from the back row was the reason for my poor grades.

Even though I knew getting glasses would solve all those problems, I didn't care. I just did not want four eyes. The last thing I needed was another reason for people to tease me.

I burst out of the nurse's office, drenched in tears. I dashed past my classmates who were waiting for various examinations. I saw some of them laughing at me. Those who weren't giggling were staring.

I didn't have time to address their ignorance or curiosity. I had to come up with a game plan. I needed a way to correct my vision without glasses. When I was in third grade, I thought eating spinach would help my eyesight. In some class we learned that taking iron sometimes strengthened eyesight. As I looked at the mirror in the girls' restroom, I realized that if my eyes were weakening, it was too late to correct them. My only hope would be to wear contact lenses. However, the thought of sticking objects in my eyes every day, and removing something from my eyes every night, was not appealing. And an operation to fix them was too scary to think about.

I turned on the faucet to sprinkle cool water on my face. Unfortunately, the water wasn't washing away my disappointment.

The door opened. I didn't want anyone to see me sobbing, so I turned my face toward the window. Footsteps approached.

"It's just me," Riana said calmly as she placed her hand on my shoulder.

"Oh, Riana," I sobbed as I turned and dropped my head in her arms.

"I figured you'd need glasses soon. I thought that back in September. Remember when there were some assignments on the board you could hardly read? Well, I took off my glasses and I couldn't see the problems either. Your headaches and mood swings were other signs. Last year when I needed glasses those things happened to me too."

She was being so understanding. So concerned. She was being a friend.

"Last week when you went to bat for me out there on the blacktop, it really meant a lot. Your actions were so surprising I didn't know how to respond. I wanted to say so many things, but nothing came out. Over Thanksgiving, when my family did our usual tradition of telling what we're thankful for, I said I was thankful for the friendship I once had with you. I thanked God for sending you and your family to Ettrick. Even though you've hurt me, I never stopped caring for you."

I was overjoyed to have my friend back. I needed her. I needed her to tell me glasses wouldn't be so bad. Riana informed me that wearing glasses actually had its perks. Having two and three pairs could be as glamorous as different pairs of earrings. She even offered to go with me to the eye doctor.

It was hard to hold back the tears. This had nothing to do with glasses. It was all about getting back something I really needed. On the first day I met her, Riana had reached out to me with real compassion. I was glad she cared enough about our bond to wait until I knew what true friendship was.

As we were coming out of the restroom, our warm moment was interrupted by Layah. She was blocking the bathroom door as if we were her prisoners. A crowd stood behind her, waiting for something to happen.

"So, Miss Browne, I hear your optical nerve is bad," she said.

"Optical nerve! What a big phrase," I said. "But do you know what it means? Let me break it down for you. *Optical* means 'good look.' And nerves allow you to feel things. Wearing glasses won't bother me, but hanging with people who judge others will upset my ability to take a good look at things and people I feel good about. You, Layah Golf, not my eyes, have deeply bothered my optical nerve."

9

Seeing Truth

Over the next two weeks, I enjoyed my black-rimmed glasses. They brought out a whole new side to my personality. I became more confident. And my desire to be intellectual returned. I wanted to study harder and learn all I could.

Writing my paper on affirmative action became my top priority. The research was fun. I watched a movie on the life of Rosa Parks and felt bad when she couldn't try on shoes in the store because of her color. I still wasn't certain what words would consume my paper, but I knew they'd come.

Riana and I started calling each other best friends. It was a title I was honored to carry. I had missed our deep talks. Our laughs. Our silliness. The Lord had given me another chance with her, and I was going to do my best not to mess this chance up.

With all the craziness surrounding my first semester at Ettrick Elementary, I hadn't had time to focus on those funny feelings I was having when I saw Spence. When Riana revealed that her feelings for Hunter were also on the back burner, we giggled endlessly. It was neat to have a close friend who understood my thoughts. Both of our bodies were changing. So we had that in common too. Although we wanted the growth to come, watching it happen was scary.

Riana and I were two ten-year-old black girls who, without the help of glasses, could not view objects clearly. Putting on the spectacles, however, gave us perfect sight. I'd quickly come to realize that my glasses were a blessing.

The following weekend, my family put up the Christmas tree. Dad placed the beautiful paper-sack black angel, adorned in a gorgeous ivory gown, on top. I knew Jesus Christ had come to earth to get rid of sin and to give us grace. Riana had given me grace by forgiving my mistake and accepting my friendship again. Wouldn't it be nice if the world had Riana's heart and Jesus' love?

✪

We were on the blacktop once again, picking teams for a kickball game. Layah refused to select me. But I didn't feel sad or timid. Riana was my buddy, and as long as we were tight, other people's acceptance didn't matter. I had to admit, though, I was a tad angry that I couldn't be a part of the game I'd grown to like a lot.

To my surprise, Spence came to my rescue. "When we played kickball two weeks ago," he said to Layah, "you had no problem with Carmen being on the team. Why does that bother you now? Don't bother answering, because there's no good reason. Besides, Miss Pryor has a rule that everyone has to participate. Don't make me report you."

Hunter joined in. "Come on, Carmen, play on our side. Too bad Riana got picked on the other team. We'd win for sure if we had her."

Out of the corner of my eye, I noticed Riana smiling. Our Prince Charmings, Hunter and Spence, wanted to hang around us because of who we were. They were no longer staying away because of who Layah said we were. Riana and I accepted their apologies.

"I won't play if Carmen plays," Layah yelled as she threw the red rubber ball on the ground. She stomped off to the pond and sat by the edge. She started throwing pebbles in the rippling water, pouting. Part of me was happy to see Layah on the sidelines for a change. But how could I be? I knew how that felt. I wouldn't wish that ugly feeling of rejection on anyone.

Lord, I prayed without closing my eyes, *help me find a way to work through the Layah issues. Only You can help. In Jesus' name, amen.*

❂

Later that night, I told Mom what had happened. She told me how proud she was that I was learning life's tough lessons and passing every course.

"You were the bigger person," she said while tucking me in bed, "not wanting to see someone else suffer. There are many blessings in that. I know that through prayer you'll be able to resolve the bitterness between you and Layah."

"I love you, Mom," I said. "I want to make you proud of me."

She stroked my hair. "I love you too, honey. Never doubt that your father and I are proud of you. We know how hard you've been working, and we believe in you. Now get some sleep."

I was happy that my parents were proud of me. Hearing her say it made me feel really special. It made me feel loved. As she kissed me on the cheek, I knew I wanted to spread that kindness to Layah. But how?

Through our family's whole move, it came to me that the Lord hadn't left my side. So I decided to pour my heart out to God. I knew He'd show me a way to make this all right.

❂

"Can I come in?" I asked while knocking on my parents' door late Wednesday night.

"Sure, honey, come on in," Dad replied.

I had racked my brain for two days trying to figure out a way that Layah and I could enjoy each other's company. Every idea I'd come up with was dumb. But I had finally found something that I thought would excite her and help us bond.

Virginia State's football team had not lost a game all season. Everyone said the huge turnaround from the previous year was because of my dad's coaching. True or not, he was the happiest he had been in years. The Trojans had earned the right to play in the Heritage Bowl, which was the black college bowl game. Morehouse College would be the opponent. The game was going to be in Maryland. The stadium they'd use was the home of the National Football League's Baltimore Ravens.

Dad was scheduled to leave the next morning. Even though the game wasn't until Saturday, the team was going to practice early. First thing Saturday, the rest of my family would drive to Baltimore. Aunt Chris and Uncle Mark were renting an eighteen-passenger van and coming from North Carolina to drive us. Clay, Cassie, and I were allowed to invite one friend each to accompany us on the journey. We were excited, not just about the big game, but about getting an opportunity to spend the night out of town as well.

My bright idea about Layah involved the trip to Baltimore. I crossed my fingers as I entered my parents' room.

"What's up, hon?" Dad asked, sitting up in the bed.

"I was thinking about the Layah incident," I started. "I know you said we can only bring one person this weekend. Riana has already agreed to go. But Layah loves sports, so I was hoping you'd allow me to take her as well."

"That's a great idea," Mom said.

My dad smiled. I gave both of my parents big hugs. Even though I didn't know if Layah would accept, I was glad I'd be able to at least ask her to join us.

In addition to getting Layah to agree, I also hoped Riana wouldn't mind. I knew I didn't need her permission, but she was my best friend. Riana deserved to be comfortable on the long trip. I had no clue if she would enjoy the journey if Layah were tagging along. Shoot, I wasn't certain I could put up with Layah.

Of all people, I believed deep down that Riana would understand. Maybe she'd even help mend the broken relationship. I didn't anticipate us being the three musketeers. However, anything was better than being archenemies.

✪

On the school bus the next morning, Riana sat beside me. I felt apprehensive about bringing up the subject of

Layah. The last thing I wanted was for Riana to back out and not go.

"Why do you keep staring at me?" Riana asked.

"Okay," I said, taking a deep breath. "I'd like for Layah to go with us this weekend to Baltimore. I haven't asked her yet, because I wanted to make sure it was okay with you first. She's not my buddy or anything. She doesn't even like me right now. But we're gonna be in school together for a long time, and being mad at someone every day isn't what I want. I'm hoping this trip can put an end to all the bitterness."

"Cool," Riana agreed without hesitation. "That's fine with me."

"You don't mind?" I replied.

"Of course not. You're my best friend, but you don't have to hang out only with me. If you want Layah to come along, maybe we can all get along."

I was really blessed to have Riana as my best friend. She didn't just say she was a Christian; anyone could see she was one.

★

Layah had been protesting kickball all week. So I knew I could find her at the pond during recess. Instead of playing the game we'd grown fond of, Riana and I sought Layah to ask her to join us for the weekend.

At first Layah didn't even turn toward us.

"Look," I blurted, tired of her attitude. "We're trying to be nice here. Can we cut out all the drama?"

She looked up at me with the saddest face. She was obviously hurting inside. I didn't dare ask her what was the matter. However, I did realize she desperately needed a friend. Maybe she could use two. Riana and I were applying for the positions. I only hoped Layah would give us the jobs. I wanted a chance at helping her work through the pain.

✪

On Saturday afternoon, Riana, Layah, and I were in a hotel room in Baltimore. Dad's team had won the big game, so the three of us were celebrating with a pillow fight. That was our way of passing the time until the victory dinner scheduled for later that evening in the hotel's ballroom. I was glad we were enjoying one another's company. We hadn't gotten into any deep conversations, but we weren't arguing either, which was definitely a step in the right direction.

All of a sudden, Layah's laughter ceased. She put down her pillow.

"What's wrong?" I asked.

"I've been so mean to you guys all semester. And you want to know my dumb reason? It's because of your glasses. The girl who fought with me on the first day of school—we fought because she made a rude comment about my mother."

Layah walked toward the hotel room window. Riana and I looked at each other, not knowing what to say or do to comfort Layah.

I didn't know much about Layah's home life. I only knew she was an only child who lived with her father. It seemed like I was about to find out much more.

"When I was four," she said, "my mother left my dad and me. She told my dad and me she was leaving us to be with some guy. The woman who gave birth to me actually said she didn't want me anymore. At the time I didn't fully understand that she was not coming back. But that's what she meant. My mother chose another man over us."

Layah explained that after her mom walked out, she became angry and bitter. As she told us her story, I saw something I never thought I'd see. Tough Layah Golf was crying. Riana gave her a tissue, and I gave her a hug.

Layah admitted she'd been wrong. She said she wanted to change her ways. The friendship among the three of us seemed like it might work after all. I was glad I had reached out. By doing so, it unleashed some of Layah's pain.

✪

At the victory dinner that evening, President Webb and Head Coach Jones called my father to the podium. My dad seemed surprised that he was being summoned to the front. When he reached the platform, both men wrapped an arm around Dad's shoulders.

President Webb announced, "Coach Jones has been the head coach for twelve years. I'm sure most of you have heard the rumor that he is going to retire. Well, I'm sad to confirm he is leaving. Coach Jones and I have proposed a successor to the board. They have unanimously agreed that we should give first crack at this job to the man standing between us. Though Coach Browne has only been a part of our program for one year, he has been instrumental in assuring us a winning program." He turned to my dad. "Coach Browne, we'd like you to be the head football coach for the Virginia State Trojans. You can think about it and get back to us tomorrow, or you can please us all by accepting the job right now."

"I've got to ask my wife," Dad stated in a shocked tone. "Honey . . ."

My mother yelled back from our table, "Go for it!"

The crowd applauded. My dad was all smiles. He had worked all his life for this dream. I was glad someone finally believed in him and his abilities enough to give him a chance to run a football program.

★

"First of all, class," Miss Pryor said on the last day before Christmas break, "I want to commend each and every one of you for doing a great job on your affirmative action papers. It was hard to select the best three. However, when I looked at spelling, grammar, structure, and content, a few papers stood out.

"Layah Golf, your paper won third place. You received a 95. James Taylor, you won second place with a 97. And our first-place paper belongs to Carmen Browne. She was the only one who based her opinion on what she thought was best for the world. She didn't focus solely on what was good for her. Carmen, you received a 100! Congratulations to all three of you." Miss Pryor handed each of us a Reebok book bag. "The principal has called a special assembly this afternoon. Since we have to go to the cafeteria in a few minutes, the winners won't have time to read their papers. So I'm passing out a sheet that has excerpts from Layah's, James's, and Carmen's papers. You can read them over the holidays or see their entire papers posted on the board."

I was blown away that my essay received first-place honors. I had worked really hard to understand affirmative action.

Before we left the classroom, we got a chance to exchange gifts. I had presents for Miss Pryor, Layah, and Riana.

"Congrats on writing the best paper," Spence said. Then, with a bashful smile, he handed me a small red box with a gold ribbon. "Here's your present. It's not much, but I wanted you to have something from me."

Accepting it, I smiled back. "Thanks a lot."

"See ya next year," he said before I could open his gift.

At the special assembly, our principal wished us a merry Christmas and a safe holiday.

Mr. Dubois, our gym teacher, approached the podium. We wondered what he had to say.

"I'll make this brief. I really enjoy working with the students and staff here and have grown to love Miss Pryor," he said. Giggles were heard all over the place. What was he doing?

Miss Pryor's mouth hung open.

"Miss Pryor, will you be my wife?"

Everyone started to cheer, and my teacher said YES.

✪

On Christmas Eve, singing carols and reading the story of baby Jesus' birth were traditions in our family. That year we were particularly happy, festive, and at peace. The move had turned out to be a blessing for all of us. Even Clay had mentioned to me that he was happy God had sent our family to love him.

My father finally had his first head-coaching job. My mother had started selling her crafts on the Internet, and they were selling like "hotcakes," as she put it. Clay found that he did like sports after all, just not football. He made the basketball team. Cassie was excited to finally step away from my shadow. She had her own friends and her own interests.

As for me—well, I learned two of the biggest lessons

of all. First, I realized I had to make the most out of wherever I went in life. Change in itself is not a bad thing. However, how you respond to your new circumstances determines whether the change is good. Secondly, I learned that to have good friends, you've got to be a good friend. And in order to be the best friend to anyone, Jesus has to be in your heart.

Dad gave me a hug. "Sorry I moved you from your old neighborhood, but I knew my tough angel would be okay."

"Yeah, I am okay, Dad," I assured him. "And thanks to you, I'm happier too."

"Now, where's that paper with the three winning excerpts?" Dad asked. "I want to read it again."

I handed my father the paper. While he read, I thought about my two new friends, Riana and Layah. I was truly happy that they were in my life. The three of us had grown a lot in a short time. I looked forward to growing more. Though I missed Jillian, God had blessed me, and I was thankful.

Dad and I sat together and silently read the essay excerpts. First, we read Layah's.

Affirmative action is definitely needed, because people still harbor prejudices toward others. I know because I was such a person. If it were not for laws that enforce equal opportunity, people who discriminate would never give chances or jobs to those who truly deserve a shot. Thanks to two new friends who cared for me, despite myself, I was able to see how wrong my actions were and how bad prejudice is.

If the people who look down on others could see their faults and change their hearts, affirmative action would not be needed. However, I don't think things will change anytime soon. When I go to look for a job, I don't want to be treated the way I have treated others—as outcasts.

Then we read James Taylor's.

Being the only white male in this class, I probably have a different viewpoint on this subject. I am against affirmative action, because those laws give white males the short end of the stick. Professional, middle management, and skilled labor positions have been taken away from people who share my color and gender, just to fill quotas. We suffer from reverse discrimination. Most of the time people who receive jobs over white males are not as qualified. If affirmative action were not in place, the best candidate would always get the opportunity.

When I get older, I don't want to be the best person for the job and not get it. I shouldn't be penalized for being a white male. After all, I can't change who I am either.

Finally, we read my excerpt.

I discriminated against a group of people this fall in order to please people in the "in crowd." Keeping others out just because I wanted them out felt good for a while. But then I had the unique experience of being placed in the group I had been discriminating against.

In this case the taboo group wore glasses. I learned that people who wear glasses are just as good as those who don't. I also learned that the ugly stigma placed on that group is unfair. Wouldn't it be awesome if everyone who held prejudice toward a particular group could become a part of the group they detest? If they became a part of that group, they would probably learn that the group was not as bad as they thought.

Regrettably, it hardly ever works that way. Males cannot change gender. Whites cannot change their skin color. Healthy people cannot know how it feels to live with a disability. So since there are people who cannot recognize the needs of others and place those needs above their own, affirmative action is desperately needed.

Affirmative action was created in 1969 under a Republican administration to help minorities receive equal opportunities. Any group being unfairly kept out deserves the chance to be placed in. I wish we all were treated equally, but we are not. I now realize prejudices are everywhere, because I'm finally seeing truth.

COMING JUNE 2005...

10-year old Carmen settles into her new home in Ettrick, Virginia. It's Christmas and Carmen has a problem. She's bored and her friends Riana and Layah are bored too. Unfortunately, their boredom turns into conspiring against their parents to have a "free day" at the mall without them. This quickly turns into a lesson on honesty and how much better it is to tell the truth than to try and deceive people, especially their parents.

Sweet Honesty
ISBN: 0-8024-8168-X
EAN/ISBN-13: 978-0-8024-8168-9

The Negro National Anthem

Lift every voice and sing
Till earth and heaven ring,
Ring with the harmonies of Liberty;
Let our rejoicing rise
High as the listening skies,
Let it resound loud as the rolling sea.
Sing a song full of the faith that the dark past has taught us,
Sing a song full of the hope that the present has brought us,
Facing the rising sun of our new day begun
Let us march on till victory is won.

So begins the Black National Anthem, written by James Weldon Johnson in 1900. Lift Every Voice is the name of the joint imprint of The Institute for Black Family Development and Moody Publishers.

Our vision is to advance the cause of Christ through publishing African-American Christians who educate, edify, and disciple Christians in the church community through quality books written for African Americans.

Since 1988, the Institute for Black Family Development, a 501(c)(3) non-profit Christian organization, has been providing training and technical assistance for churches and Christian organizations. The Institute for Black Family Development's goal is to become a premier trainer in leadership development, management, and strategic planning for pastors, ministers, volunteers, executives, and key staff members of churches and Christian organizations. To learn more about The Institute for Black Family Development write us at:

15151 Faust
Detroit, Michigan 48223

Since 1894, *Moody Publishers* has been dedicated to equip and motivate people to advance the cause of Christ by publishing evangelical Christian literature and other media for all ages, around the world. Because we are a ministry of the Moody Bible Institute of Chicago, a portion of the proceeds from the sale of this book go to train the next generation of Christian leaders. If we may serve you in any way in your spiritual journey toward understanding Christ and the Christian life, please contact us at:

820 N. LaSalle Blvd.
Chicago, Illinois 60610
www.moodypublishers.com

TRUE FRIENDS TEAM

ACQUIRING EDITOR
Cynthia Ballenger

BACK COVER COPY
Lisa Ann Cockrel

COPY EDITOR
Tanya Harper

COVER DESIGN
Lydell Jackson, JaXon Communications

INTERIOR DESIGN
Ragont Design

PRINTING AND BINDING
Color House Graphics

The typeface for the text of this book is
Berkeley